‖‖‖‖‖‖‖‖‖‖‖‖‖‖‖‖‖‖‖‖
W9-AMT-540

DINO DETECTIVE
AND
AWESOME POSSUM

PRIVATE EYES

THE CASE
OF THE NIBBLED
PIZZA

by Tadgh Bentley

Penguin Workshop

For Fionn

PENGUIN WORKSHOP
An Imprint of Penguin Random House LLC, New York

Penguin supports copyright. Copyright fuels creativity, encourages diverse voices, promotes free speech, and creates a vibrant culture. Thank you for buying an authorized edition of this book and for complying with copyright laws by not reproducing, scanning, or distributing any part of it in any form without permission. You are supporting writers and allowing Penguin to continue to publish books for every reader.

Copyright © 2021 by Penguin Random House LLC. All rights reserved. Published by Penguin Workshop, an imprint of Penguin Random House LLC, New York. PENGUIN and PENGUIN WORKSHOP are trademarks of Penguin Books Ltd, and the W colophon is a registered trademark of Penguin Random House LLC. Manufactured in China.

Visit us online at www.penguinrandomhouse.com.

Library of Congress Cataloging-in-Publication Data is available upon request.

ISBN 9780593093498 (paperback)   10 9 8 7 6 5 4 3 2 1
ISBN 9780593093481 (library binding)   10 9 8 7 6 5 4 3 2 1

CHAPTER ONE
THE CRIME

It was a normal day in the town of Berp. The sun was high in the sky, and a gentle breeze carried the sound of a lawn mower through Awesome Possum's open window. He was having a wonderful dream, riding through space on Mr. Timms, and eating delicious pizza. The space breeze blew through his fur and—

"Wake up, Awesome Possum!"
Awesome Possum woke up to find
an upset T. rex sitting on his feet.
    "Possum, wake up! We have a case!
A big case!"

2

It was his sister, Dino Detective, crack investigator and one half of Dino Detective and Awesome Possum, Private Eyes. The agency was a dynamite team of brother-sister private eyes, a dynamic duo of mystery solvers, always on the hunt for a new case.

But right now, one half of the agency did not want to get up. The thought of a big case would normally make Possum jump straight out of bed, but recently, Dino had raised a few false alarms.

Like the time that she thought she had FINALLY discovered evidence of aliens. (Mrs. Saunders, as it turned out, was a narwhal, *not* an alien.)

Or the time that she had thought Bigfoot was a shoe thief. (Bigfoot, apparently, had no interest in stealing Possum's tiny shoes.)

"What IS it, Dino?"

"This is big, Possum, this is serious. Grandma Thunderclaps's delicious Sicilian pizza—it's, it's…" Dino took a moment to compose herself.

4

"IT'S BEEN EATEN!" Dino sobbed.

"Eaten?!"

"Well," said Dino, "more *nibbled* than eaten."

Still, thought Awesome Possum, *this could be a case. This could be THE case, the one that finally puts the agency on the map.*

His blanket flew into the air as he jumped out of bed. Dino grabbed Plant, and they raced down to the kitchen.

Here we go again...

Everything looked normal…

…except the pizza. From a distance, it didn't seem like there was anything unusual. But as Possum got closer, he could see that Dino was right—it was covered in small nibbles. But even worse than the nibbling was the pepperoni. It was completely gone.

Who would do such a thing?

Who would commit such a terrible crime?

Dino Detective and Awesome Possum looked at each other with just one thought on their minds.

This sounded like a case for:

Dino
Detective
and
Awesome
Possum
PRIVATE EYES

CHAPTER TWO

THE AGENCY

I know this is unusual,
to hear from a plant,
but you are reading a book
about a talking dinosaur
with a possum for a
brother, whose
grandmother's pizza
has just been
mysteriously nibbled.
So let's just go with it.

These masterminds clearly think that this is a big deal, especially since they don't get too many big deals. Dino Detective and Awesome Possum have been "investigating" "crimes" since they were knee-high to a dandelion. There has been no case too big for the agency, no case too small.

Which is just as well, because they tend to get a lot of small cases—generally lots of missing things, with the occasional whodunit.

But each one has somehow demanded their full attention.

CASE 3: WHERE ARE MOM'S CAR KEYS?

CASE 16: WHO ATE DINO'S CANDY?

CASE 24: WHO'S EATING THE BIRD FOOD?

Dino has lots of ideas, some of them quite brilliant. But she tends to get a little...distracted.

Possum is different. He's sharp and focused, just like their favorite TV character—Butch Malone. They are obsessed with him.

He has this TV show, *Butch Malone, Private Eye*, where he spends his time tracking down bad guys and solving crimes, all in the Big City. Do these people know how filthy the Big City is?

No self-respecting plant would go there: It's just buildings and concrete everywhere.

No comfy, soft soil, no clean flowing water, and just *imagine* the germs there. Ugh.

Anyway. These fools seem to think that Berp is a town chock-full of master criminals, and it is only a matter of time before they land a BIG CASE.

And they think this is it.

There's just one thing. I know who did it. I've been watching the whole time.

CHAPTER THREE
WHODUNIT?

Do you see what I have to work with here?

Dino looked over the scene. "Okay, Possum. I think it is clear what has happened here. The pepperoni has obviously grown legs and walked off. It's finally happened. Now, where would it have walked to?"

"Hang on, Dino, there is more to it than that. Pepperoni doesn't grow legs and walk off. Someone has eaten it."

14

"But who?"

"Butch Malone always says that the most likely suspects are people the victim knew."

Dino's mind buzzed with possibilities, but she quickly shook them away. "It's a pizza, Possum, not a victim. It didn't *know* anyone."

"You know what I mean. Who would have eaten it? Could it be someone from home?"

Possum and Dino eyed each other warily.

"Well, *I* didn't eat it," huffed Dino. "Why do you think I'm so hungry? I haven't eaten anything all afternoon!"

Possum took out his pencil and scribbled down some possible suspects in his notepad.

SUSPECT: Grandma Thunderclaps
PROS:
☑ maker of pizza
☑ last one to see pizza whole
CONS
☒ centaurs are strict vegetarians CLEARED

SUSPECT: Possum
PROS:
☑ loves pizza
☑ loves pepperoni
☑ small bite
CONS
☒ asleep all afternoon CLEARED

SUSPECT: Dino
PROS:
☑ loves pizza
☑ always hungry
CONS:
☒ bite size too big
☒ was playing checkers with plant all afternoon CLEARED

Suspect: Plant

PROS:
☑ ummm...

CONS
☒ not known for eating stuff
☒ or being able to move
☒ is a plant CLEARED

It wasn't anyone from the house. They would need to think bigger, think wider. There was a whole town out there. Someone was hiding a secret, a lie, and a taste for pizza. Who could it possibly be?

They needed to do some detective work.

CHAPTER FOUR
CLUES

Dino rushed around the crime scene, hoping for a clear sign of a break-in. But there were no muddy footprints or overturned chairs, no smashed doors or crowbars left lying around. There wasn't even a ransom note demanding money.

Awesome Possum combed for clues and took out his notebook.

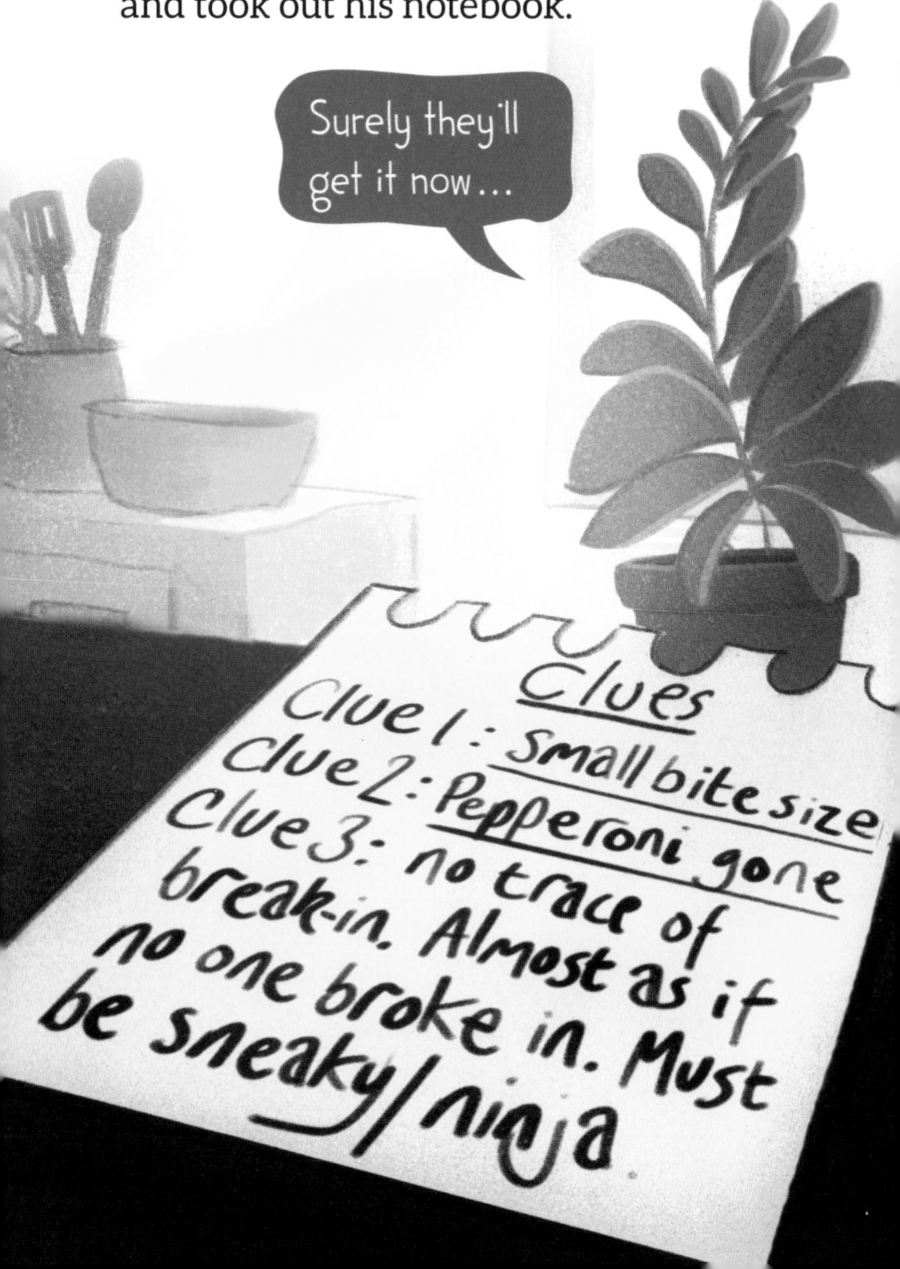

Surely they'll get it now...

Clues
Clue 1: Small bite size
Clue 2: Pepperoni gone
Clue 3: no trace of break-in. Almost as if no one broke in. Must be sneaky/ninja

Possum and Dino used the clues to make a new list of suspects who WEREN'T family members. One name appeared on all of them: Nibbles McSqueak.

small bite size
Peeps von Teeney
Lucian Drabbernackle
Bruno Shortstaff
LongLegs McSweeney
Nibbles McSqueak
Little Tony

Pepperoni lover
Big Tony
Little Lila
Nibbles McSqueak
The ~lo ch
Hoots O'Hallahan
Lucille Stompberry

Sneaky
Cliff Elvin
Blunderbus McNairy
Toots McGraw
Nibbles McSqueak
Dr. Splatt

Nibbles was a mouse from Possum's grade at school. He had the right bite size, and mice were well known for being sneaky *and* loving cheesy pepperoni pizza. But was he a thief?

"Right!" said Dino. "It's Nibbles! We go straight to the police, they lock him up, and then I can finally eat the evidence."

"No, Dino. We cannot go to the police, not after last time. They won't take us seriously."

"That wasn't my fault! I was certain that ninja had stolen my shoes!"

"That 'ninja' was a porcupine! Other people wear black shoes, too! Give it a rest, Dino!"

"Then what do we do?"

Possum thought back to his favorite
Butch Malone episodes. If Butch
suspected someone of a crime, did he
run straight to the police? No. He found
the suspect, watched his movements,
collected evidence. That sort of thing.

"We need to find Nibbles. We need to watch his movements, collect evidence… that sort of thing," Possum said confidently.

"Then we can eat pizza?"

"Yes, Dino. Then we can eat pizza. But first, we've got a case to crack."

Across the room, Plant gazed out
the window. Possum thought he heard
a long, frustrated sigh, but it must have
been the wind.

CHAPTER FIVE

NIBBLES
MCSQUEAK

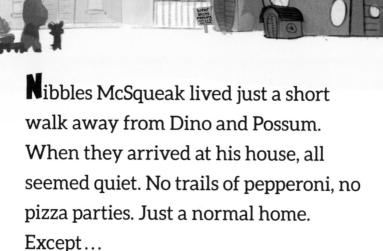

Nibbles McSqueak lived just a short
walk away from Dino and Possum.
When they arrived at his house, all
seemed quiet. No trails of pepperoni, no
pizza parties. Just a normal home.
Except…

… they heard hushed voices coming from inside the garage. Possum moved closer. "What's going on in there?"

"I say we bust right in, catch them in the act," said Dino excitedly.

"We don't even know what we would be catching them at. We can't just barge in. We need to do some detective work."

Dino saw some windows high on the garage wall. They scrambled up some boxes and looked in.

"Look, Possum. Pizza!"

Possum looked closer. "Yes, but all cheese toppings—no pepperoni. Shh... let's listen."

The mice at the table were listening intently to a larger, older mouse.

"Everything is coming together perfectly for our master plan," said the large mouse. "Mikey, where are we with the fireworks?"

SUPER SECRET PLAN 6B

PIZZA

P·ZZA

P·ZZA

P·ZZA

P·ZZA

"We're good, Boss. I'll have boxes down at the launch site by midnight."

The large mouse went on. "Nibbles, you got the goods?"

Well, blow me over with a breeze!

Possum's ears pricked up. They looked on as Nibbles stepped out from the shadows, brought a bag forward, and placed it on the table for all to see.

"It could be our pepperoni!" whispered Possum.

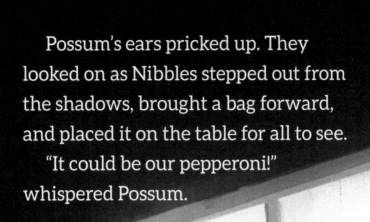

Or it could be an *actual* crime...

"It was difficult, Boss," said Nibbles, "but we did it."

Nibbles went to open the bag.

A hush filled the room. The mice leaned in, eager to get a look. Dino and Possum struggled to see. Even Plant was curious...

It wasn't the pepperoni.

"Me and Tony Four Fingers spent the whole afternoon in a *drama* class. You know Tony don't do that stuff, Boss, but he played the part. We got 'em."

"*What* are they doing with those?" asked Dino.

"Drama class?" whispered Possum. "Nibbles said he was there the whole afternoon."

"That's a pretty solid alibi."

The large mouse continued talking, "Excellent, boys, excellent. These costumes will be the perfect disguises for our raid. Noodles, how are the numbers coming?"

"Looking good, Boss. My numbers are telling me it shouldn't take more than an hour to reach our target. We will use Big Bertha to haul back the stolen goods."

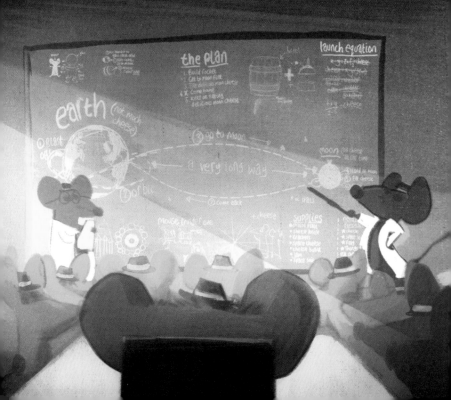

The large mouse looked around, satisfied. "You done good, boys, real good. No one can stop us now, no one even knows what we're planning. But by the end of tonight, they'll know. Oh boy, will they know."

From outside the window, Dino shot a look at Possum. "No one can stop them? No one knows what's happening? Are you thinking what I'm thinking?"

Possum nodded seriously. "I think so... Mice. Disguises. Fireworks. Some kind of secret plot? This has absolutely *nothing* to do with our pepperoni."

"Right. This is a waste of time! Calculations? Stolen goods? We've got a *serious* crime to investigate."

Plant looked on, and again let out a long, quiet sigh.

CHAPTER SIX

THE PIZZA THICKENS

With no sign of their pepperoni, Dino and Possum were turning to go when out of nowhere… a figure appeared.

She simply popped into existence—one moment she wasn't there, and the next, she was. Luckily for her, the mice were too busy stuffing their snouts with pizza to notice.

"Mrs. Sniffleton?" whispered a confused Dino. "What's *she* doing here?" Mrs. Sniffleton was a friendly lunch lady at school.

Dino and Possum watched as she quickly ducked under the table, then carefully rummaged through boxes. Spotting the papers on the table, she grabbed a pile and stuffed them into her bag.

"What's she doing with those?" wondered Possum.

Watching the mice closely, Mrs. Sniffleton reached out and grabbed a slice of pizza. Slice in hand, she then promptly vanished into thin air, leaving no trace behind.

Well, *almost* no trace. As she disappeared, something fell to the ground.

Dino sprang into action. "What are you *doing*?" hissed Possum. "Wait!"

But Dino had already clambered down the boxes and disappeared around the corner.

Possum watched in horror as Dino opened the side door and slipped inside the garage. She made her way slowly along the back wall, inching silently toward the mysterious object. She reached down and picked it up.

Through the window, Possum pointed frantically back toward the door, and put a finger to his lips. Dino needed to be totally silent to get out without anyone noticing. Dino looked up, nodded at Possum...

… and ran for it.

Tables toppled as Dino went smashing through the garage, boxes scattering this way and that. Possum watched, horrified, as startled mice stopped munching and looked over at the racket. A few began scurrying in Dino's direction, just as she made her exit.

The mice were fast, but they were no match for an escaping T. rex. Dino zoomed around the street corner, leaving a trail of mice in her wake.

Possum, safe from all the confusion, quietly climbed down the boxes and headed in the other direction. They needed a serious agency discussion.

CHAPTER SEVEN

I HAVE A
BAD FEELING
ABOUT THIS

"**W**hat were you *thinking*?!" asked Possum when they finally met up. "You were supposed to *sneak* out, not smash through walls like Godzilla!"

"I thought you were telling me to be quick!" cried Dino. "Besides. That thing she dropped! It could be a clue! You saw Mrs. Sniffleton take their pizza; maybe *she* took our pepperoni."

"Just because she took a slice of their pizza doesn't mean that she ate our pepperoni."

"Look at your notes, Possum. She fits all the clues! You saw her appear and disappear—she could have gotten in and out of our house without leaving a trace. She's the right size. She obviously loves pizza. She's a prime suspect!"

Possum had to admit that it did look rather strange. "What did she drop?"

Dino's mind whirred as she looked down at the clue. What *was* Mrs. Sniffleton doing in the garage? Why did she take those papers? Why did she have this flower?

The flower … The more Dino thought about it, the more familiar it looked. "Possum. This flower is from that tree in the park."

"There are a lot of trees in the park, Dino."

"I mean *that* tree. The one planted last year to celebrate Mr. Jones winning World's Best Mustache. We need to go there, right now."

The park was just a few blocks away from their house. Mr. Jones's tree really was an impressive sight. It was unusual because of its large size and odd shape, but that wasn't the only thing that made it unique. Every branch was covered in bright purple flowers that bloomed all summer. The same purple, in fact, as Mrs. Sniffleton's flower.

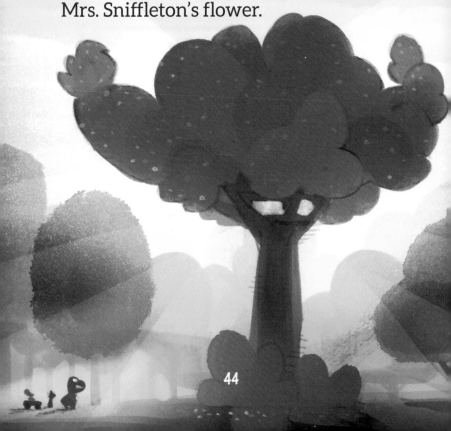

"I thought I recognized it!" said Dino. "The flower *is* from this tree. It's the only one like it in town."

They searched the area. No clues on the ground, which left only one place to look.

"Time to start climbing, Dino."

High in the canopy, they found a small tree house.

Keeping quiet, they peeked in through a window and spotted a figure speaking into a phone, deep in conversation. *Mrs. Sniffleton.*

"You were right, sir. My years in deep
cover have all been worth it. I've got
their plans."

They heard a muffled voice on the
other end of the line.

"It's worse than we thought, though.
I can't believe I missed it. It's like I've been
sleepwalking through the investigation
this whole time. It's tonight. Their rocket
is ready, and they've got their disguises."

"Ugh. She's talking about the mice," said Dino.

"There is one more thing," continued Mrs. Sniffleton. "As I was leaving, it was mayhem. Someone was crashing through that joint like a tornado in a greenhouse."

Possum glared at Dino.

"Not sure. But whoever it was, my cover was nearly blown. Must have been a real professional."

Dino smiled smugly back at Possum.

"I'm quite sure, sir. I kept watch all day. I was starving by the time I left. Had to take a slice of their pizza to keep me going."

Possum locked eyes with Dino. "Did you hear what she said?"

"About me being a real professional?"

"Not that! She said that she didn't leave the garage *all day.*"

"Another alibi." Dino sighed.

"This has nothing to do with our pepperoni, either," said Possum.

"But, Possum, doesn't this stuff with the mice sound... just a bit... suspicious?"

"We've got to stay focused, Dino. Think: What would Butch Malone do? This pepperoni is our one chance at a BIG case. You want to drop it for mice and lunch ladies?"

"You're right. Let's go. We've got work to do."

As they got to the ground, something caught Dino's eye.

A single, beautiful slice of pizza. The fading sunlight shone on the gooey cheese topping. Dino licked her lips.

Oh, this does not look good.

"Pizza!" she exclaimed, heading toward the slice.

"Wait, wait!" hushed Possum. "Dino, you shouldn't…"

The smell of the cheese. The crispiness of the crust. All of it was too much for Dino, who charged toward her prey with Possum trailing behind.

"Dino! For once, will you just stop and w—"

But it was too late. Possum heard a faint snapping sound, followed by a rustle of leaves and a *whooosh!*

And all went black.

CHAPTER EIGHT
MRS. SNIFFLETON

> Trapped! I, Plant, captured?! In a bag? This thing is **filthy!**

Caught! Like a mouse in a trap. Or a possum and a dinosaur in a big canvas bag.

They heard a flutter of wings, and then the bag was opened, and they were dumped out. In front of them hovered Mrs. Sniffleton.

She did not look happy.

"Who are you? What are you doing here?" asked the lunch lady. "Talk! Are you working for the mice?"

"No, we aren't working for the mice!" huffed Possum. "We're trying to catch a thief!"

"And what are YOU doing setting traps for hungry, innocent dinosaurs?!" added Dino.

"A thief?!" cried Mrs. Sniffleton. "What thief?"

"Someone snuck into our house and ate all the pepperoni, so we've been hunting around the entire town looking for clues but we aren't getting anywhere and I'm REALLY HUNGRY!" cried Dino.

"Pepperoni?" Mrs. Sniffleton's brow wrinkled in a deep frown. "Those mice are on the verge of the crime of the century… and you are worried about… pepperoni?"

An alarm bell went off.

"What is that?" asked Dino.

Mrs. Sniffleton didn't have time to answer. A canvas bag, very similar to the one that had trapped Possum, Dino, and Plant, zoomed up through a trapdoor. The figures in the bag did not sound happy.

More alarms went off, and then suddenly a mouse in a clown costume flew through an open window. Its giant floppy clown feet made it trip as soon as it hit the floor.

"We're onto you, Sniffleton!" cried an alien mouse as it burst through a different window. "We know you were in the garage!"

An Egyptian mummy mouse fell through the ceiling. "Give us the plans, Sniffleton, there's no use fighting!" But Mrs. Sniffleton clearly wasn't in the mood for talking. With swift karate chops, she dinged the clown and sent the mummy flying across the room. She grabbed the plans and stuffed them into her bag.

More mice came pouring in through the open window, mice dressed as ghosts, superheroes, wizards, and witches. All were grasping at Mrs. Sniffleton's bag. Just as it seemed like they would get it, she furrowed her brow and disappeared.

The mice fell to the floor…

… and all looked up at Dino and Possum, who were too stunned by the cast of costumed characters to have really moved at all.

Well, I never…

But now they moved. Possum grabbed Plant and jumped on Dino's back, and Dino made her trademark exit. They scrambled down the branches, leaving mummies, clowns, and aliens in their wake.

CHAPTER NINE

NO CLUES LEFT

When they felt like they were far enough away from the tree, Dino slowed down, and Possum jumped off to walk by her side with Plant. "Well, there is only one thing to do now," said Possum.

Eat pizza, thought Dino. *Lots of pizza.* "I'm thinking the same thing, Possum. We need to eat. Then we can get back on the case."

After a full afternoon on the case, Possum was tired. He had seen enough pizza-stealing fairies and costumed mice. "I've had enough for tonight, Dino. I want to go home."

"Home?" asked Dino. "We finally get a BIG CASE, and you want to give up? All we need is a quick snack, and then back to it."

"Back to what?" snapped Possum. "We have no more leads, no more ideas. I know YOU would like to run blindly into the night, but I'm tired, Dino! I've been chasing you around all day! Maybe if you had STOPPED to THINK for a minute before smashing through walls and falling into traps, we might have solved the case already!"

If I had stopped and thought more, we wouldn't have gotten as far as we have!"

"Fine! I'm going home!"

With that, Possum stomped off toward home, and Dino was left alone. She wondered about continuing the investigation on her own. But Possum was right. She had no leads, no clues to follow. Reluctantly, she headed back home.

As soon as she walked in, Dino immediately thought about eating the evidence, but thought that would probably make Possum even more angry.

Instead, she went upstairs to find Possum already in bed, sound asleep and snoring loudly. In spite of her rumbling tummy, Dino had to admit that she was sleepy, too.

But when she lay down, her mind
spun with thoughts about the case.
The pepperoni, the mice, Mrs.
Sniffleton. One thing in particular
kept playing over in Dino's mind. Mrs.
Sniffleton had mentioned something
about sleepwalking through the
investigation.

Sleepwalking?

Investigation?

Possum?

Dino drifted off to sleep.

65

YOU DUNNIT

At first, Dino thought that the sounds were coming from her stomach. But as she slowly woke up, she realized that it was less a gurgling and rumbling and more a clanging and chomping.

And it was coming from downstairs.

"Wake up, Possum!" hissed Dino. "The thief is back to finish the job!"

But Possum did not respond, not

Dino had to do something. She picked up Plant for backup and crept downstairs, ready to catch the thief in the act.

As she approached the door of the kitchen, she heard more chewing and chomping. She peered inside and saw that the fridge *was* open. A shadowy figure stood at the fridge door, rummaging around.

"No, Mr. Timms, that is *my* slice…," muttered the figure groggily.

Mr. Timms? thought Dino. *He's in on it, too?*

Not quite sure how she thinks I'm supposed to help here.

Dino was ready to pounce.
She wished that Possum were here.
But what would Possum do? He would
tell her to wait and watch, to gather
information. But this was no time to
wait. It was time for action. The figure
stepped away from the fridge, with a
large slice of Grandma Thunderclaps's
pizza in its paws.

"GOTCHA!" Pizza flew into the air, and Dino tumbled to the floor with the flailing thief.

A struggle! A real, Butch Malone–like struggle! There was rolling and grasping and an awful lot of confusion. Dino struggled to grab a pizza slice from the thief's hands...

... but wait a sec, these hands seemed familiar...

"Possum!?"

Possum looked up groggily at Dino. "Dino? What's going on?"

"I was about to ask you the same question. You're supposed to be asleep, remember. Thought you'd help yourself to a midnight treat instead?"

Dino looked suspiciously at Possum.
She'd caught him red-handed, paws
deep in the pizza. But something didn't
add up. This didn't sound like something
Possum would do…

Unless…

FINALLY!

72

Dino realized why she couldn't get Mrs. Sniffleton's words out of her head. Suddenly, it all became clear.

"Possum! It was you! *You* are the pepperoni thief!"

"What? What are you talking about? It couldn't have been me! I was asleep the whole afternoon."

"Exactly! You said you were dreaming. Do you remember what you were dreaming about?"

"Mr. Timms! We were flying through space, eating pizz—"

Possum looked down at his pizza-covered hands.

He could taste the pizza sauce slathered all over his pizza-covered face.

Could it be true? The dream that afternoon had been so real, so vivid. At least, he *thought* it had been a dream…

"Sleepwalking!" cried Dino. "It was you! You must have come down here this afternoon, eaten the pizza, and then gone back to bed. All while asleep. It explains the bites, it explains why there was no sign of anyone else. And you do particularly like pepperoni."

"You've done it, Dino! You solved the crime!"

"*We've* done it!" cried Dino. "We cracked the case! It's a good thing we didn't get distracted by those mice. What *were* they doing, anyway?"

"Never mind, Dino. Whatever it was, we didn't have time, not when there was such serious detective work to do."

EPILOGUE

The next morning, Possum woke to a familiar smell drifting up from the kitchen. He stumbled sleepily downstairs to find Dino sitting at the kitchen table with Dad, and Grandma Thunderclaps pulling something out of the oven.

"Good morning, dears!" said Grandma. "Fresh pizza, just for you!"

Possum sat down, ready to munch. Dad didn't look up from his paper. "Morning, Possum. Have you read the news this morning? Crazy goings-on in town last night. Apparently, the town's mice were…"

Something caught Possum's eye as he tuned Dad out.

"Dino, why are you only wearing one sock?" Possum asked.

"…and they would have gotten away with it if your school lunch lady hadn't…," Dad continued, uninterrupted.

"It's all I've got left," answered Dino,

chomping on pizza. "It's funny. I keep losing socks, but only one at a time."

Dad carried on. "But still, no one knows *why*. It's some kind of huge mystery."

Possum froze. His mind whirred with the magnitude of what was happening (and it was also quite difficult to tune out the droning on of his father).

Possum's socks had been mysteriously vanishing, too.

Aaand... here we go again...

Every day it seemed that he found a newly single sock in his drawer. It had been happening for weeks now. Could it be a coincidence that they were both losing socks? Surely not.

But who would do such a thing?

Who would commit such a terrible crime?

This sounded like a case for:

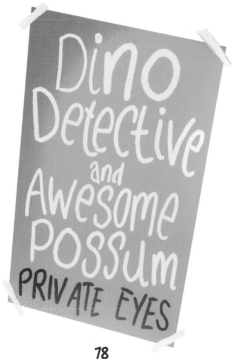